DISCARDED

Meet the DULLARDS

BY Sara Pennypacker   ILLUSTRATED BY Daniel Salmieri

BALZER + BRAY
An Imprint of HarperCollins Publishers

For David, definitely never dull . . .
—S.P.

For Uncle Mark, Aunt Terry, and Cousin Michael—
the opposites of the Dullards.
—D.S.

Balzer + Bray is an imprint of HarperCollins Publishers.

Meet the Dullards
Text copyright © 2015 by Sara Pennypacker
Illustrations copyright © 2015 by Daniel Salmieri
All rights reserved. Manufactured in China.
No part of this book may be used or reproduced in any manner whatsoever
without written permission except in the case of brief quotations embodied in
critical articles and reviews. For information address HarperCollins Children's
Books, a division of HarperCollins Publishers, 195 Broadway, New York, NY 10007.
www.harpercollinschildrens.com

Library of Congress Cataloging-in-Publication Data
Pennypacker, Sara, date.
    Meet the Dullards / by Sara Pennypacker ; illustrated by Daniel Salmieri. —
First edition.
          pages   cm
    Summary: "Mr. and Mrs. Dullard move their family to a boring town to
avoid any excitment in their lives"— Provided by publisher.
    ISBN 978-0-06-219856-3 (hardcover)
    [1. Family life—Fiction.   2. Moving, Household—Fiction.   3. Humorous
stories.]   I. Salmieri, Daniel, date. illustrator.   II. Title.
PZ7.P3856Dr   2014   2013037321
[E]—dc23   CIP
                                                                    AC

The artist used watercolor, gouache, and colored pencil on paper to create the
illustrations for this book.
Typography by Dana Fritts
14 15 16 17 18   SCP   10 9 8 7 6 5 4 3 2 1
❖ First Edition

One day, Mr. and Mrs. Dullard received quite a nasty surprise.

The Dullards collected the books and handed their children some nice blank paper to read instead. Then they left the room to discuss the problem in private.

This was not the first time their children had given them a shock. Last week, they had asked to go to school. And just the day before, Mr. Dullard had caught them trying to play outside.

Mrs. Dullard shook her head sadly.
"Where did we go wrong?"
"Now, now," Mr. Dullard comforted his wife.
"It can't be our fault . . . we're perfectly dull.

"Perhaps it's this place," he said. "Last fall, remember, some leaves turned color. And now this. . . ." He pointed to an upsetting commotion in the driveway. "There's never a dull moment."

"You may be right. It's like a circus around here," Mrs. Dullard agreed. "This is no place to raise Blanda, Borely, and Little Dud."

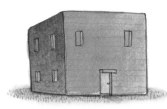  

So the Dullards packed up their three dull children
and all their dull things and moved.

Just as they brought the last box into their new home, a lady
came to the door. "Welcome to the neighborhood," she said.
"I baked you an applesauce cake!"

"Please don't use exclamation marks in front of our children,"
said Mrs. Dullard.

"Smooth or chunky applesauce?" asked Mr. Dullard. "Chunks are
so unpredictable. So nerve-racking."

"I'm sorry," said the neighbor lady. "It was chunky."

"Good-bye," said the Dullards, shutting the door.

"Well, I never . . . ," they heard the neighbor lady muttering
as she carried her cake away.

"Well, we never either," said Mr. Dullard. "That's how we
keep our family so dull."

"You children need to calm down after all that excitement,"
said Mrs. Dullard. "Go watch the television."

Mr. and Mrs. Dullard finished unpacking all their dull things. "Ah, this place feels more boring already," said Mr. Dullard.

But then . . .

On the way to the paint store, the Dullards spotted an ice-cream stand. Mr. Dullard ordered their usual. "Five vanilla cones, please. Hold the cones. And extract the vanilla."

"But all that would be left is plain ice cream," the clerk said.

"Yes, that's correct," said Mr. Dullard.

At the paint store, Mr. Dullard suggested a medium gray.

"Too risky," Mrs. Dullard decided. "Gray is the color of highways, and highways could make the children think about going somewhere. How about beige?"

"Out of the question," said her husband. "Beige reminds me of clay. The children might think of that and"—he put his hand to his heart—"want to make something."

In the end, they told the clerk to mix the gray paint and the beige paint together, and the new color was indeed perfectly dull—like oatmeal left in the pot.

After they finished painting the room, Mr. and
Mrs. Dullard tried not to look at the walls. But
it was no use—they were completely mesmerized.
All day long, the Dullards watched the paint dry.

Finally, Mr. Dullard tore his gaze away. "I think—" he began.

Mrs. Dullard shook her head. "No thinking," she reminded her husband. "It sets a bad example for the children."

"And speaking of the children . . . where are they?"

"I can't imagine what came over them," Mr. Dullard said as he herded the children safely back inside. "Perhaps it's this new home. It's terribly exciting."
"You may be right. It's like a circus around here," Mrs. Dullard agreed.
"This is no place to raise Blanda, Borely, and Little Dud."

So the Dullards packed up their three
dull children and all their dull things . . .

and moved back.

That night, Mr. and Mrs. Dullard fell asleep right away,
secure in the knowledge that their children were perfect bores.

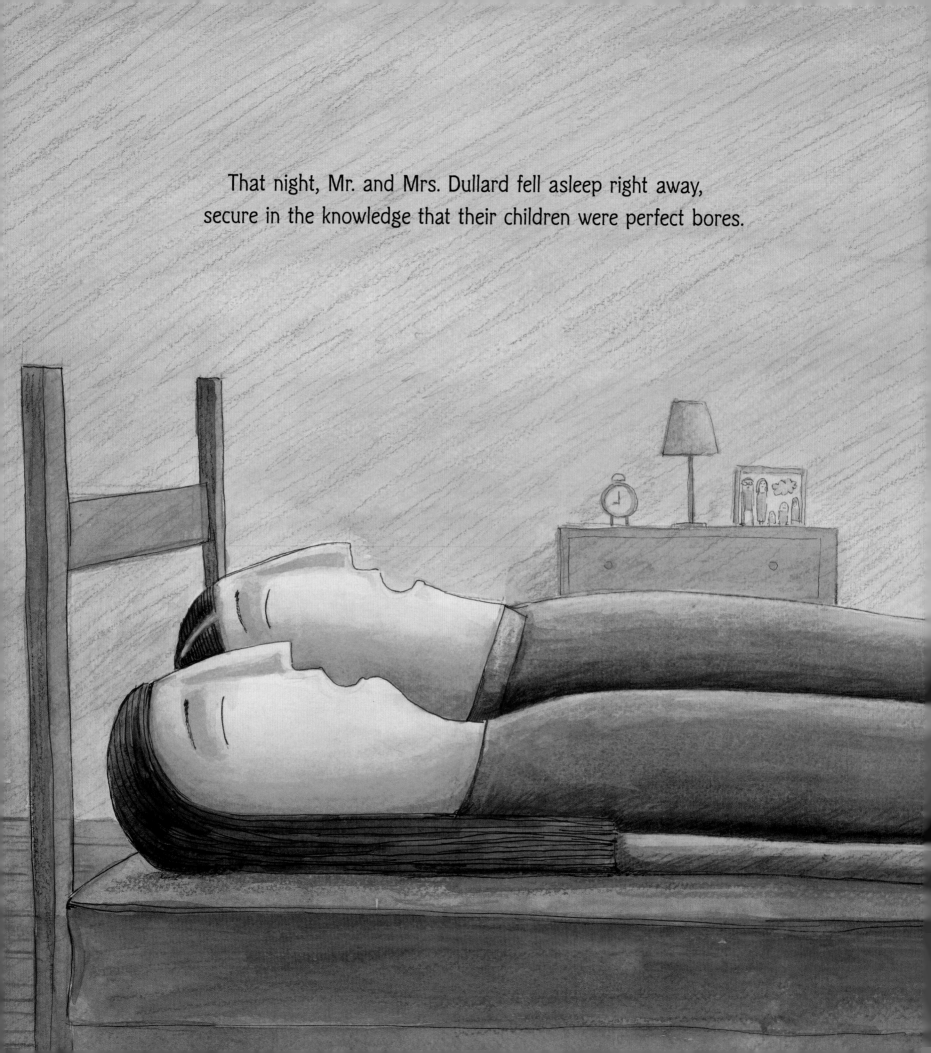